ADVENTURES OF AN ADORABLE FAT GIRL

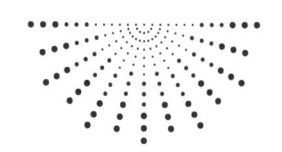

BERNICE BLOOM

WELCOME TO MY NEW BOOK...

Hello,

Thank you so much for downloading book two in the Adorable Fat Girl series which continues the adventures of the delicious, larger-than-life, Mary Brown. In this book we learn how far the lovely Mary will go for love, and just how much trouble two women can get into when let loose in Amsterdam (errr...lots!).

I really hope you enjoy reading about our delightful, overweight heroine.

Thank you so much for your support.

Lots of love, Bernice xx

COPYRIGHT

Published internationally by Gold Medals Media Ltd:

Bernice Bloom 2018

Terms and Conditions:

The purchaser of this book is subject to the condition that he/she shall in no way resell it, nor any part of it, nor make copies of it to distribute freely.

All Persons Fictitious Disclaimer:

This book is a work of fiction. Any similarity between the characters and situations within its pages and places or persons, living or dead, is unintentional and coincidental.

1. WILL ANYONE EVER MAKE A FASHIONABLE, FLATTERING DRESS THAT FITS ME?

There is nothing on earth quite like the terror felt by a large woman in a public changing room trapped inside a small dress.

And, ladies and gentlemen, I speak as someone who knows, because that large woman was me. I don't know quite how it happened; one minute I was inching my way into a lacy, black skater dress; the next I was completely stuck; unable to extricate myself from it.

I knew the dress would be tight on me before I started putting it on, but I was convinced that if I just wriggled around it would fit. I had no idea it would be this tight, with the material stretching as if it might tear completely at any moment. Oh God. The whole thing was bursting at the seams.

"Everything is OK?" came a voice from outside the cubicle. It was the skinny, dark-haired assistant who I'd swept passed earlier.

I froze in terror.

"All fine," I said. But that was a lie… I wasn't fine. I was well and truly stuck. But I couldn't tell her that.

"You manage to get on?" she asked in a soft Spanish accent.

I put my foot against the door.

"Yes, all fine. I've got the dress on."

And, to be fair, that was the truth – I had got the damn thing on. I had managed to squeeze it over my vast bosom and had forced my big arms into the lace sleeves. What was proving much more difficult was getting it off.

I looked at myself in the mirror; I looked like an overstuffed black-pudding.

I tried pulling at the sleeves but they wouldn't budge at all. They were made of lace so I was terrified to yank too hard in case the whole thing fell apart in front of me. I tried lifting the dress over my head but the bodice part of the skater dress was staying tight on my body and the zip was stuck fast.

I waited until I heard the assistant leave and called out to my friend Veronica, hovering outside the door waiting to see me emerge, looking delicious and gorgeous in a little black dress.

"Veronica, get in here quickly, I'm stuck."

"What do you mean 'you're stuck'?"

Veronica walked in.

"Oh blimey, you're stuck." She smirked, then saw my beetroot red face and flustered disposition and thought better than to laugh at my predicament.

"This stupid dress is way too small, and it won't come off," I said. "It's a complete nightmare."

"They have a really odd sizing policy here," said Veronica supportively. "Even really skinny girls find the clothes small. It's not your fault."

In truth, I suspected they had a perfectly reasonable sizing policy. It was my eating policy that was all wrong.

She suggested that the only way to remove the dress was from the bottom up, so she lifted the skirt of the dress to try and get it over my chest.

"It won't go," I warned her. She pulled so hard that I feared she might take half my internal organs with her. But still, the dress wouldn't budge. Veronica continued to pull, baring her teeth she yanked at the material with all her might and I pushed back with all mine.

"Try taking the dress from the arms," I suggested. "But be careful with the lace."

Veronica moved her hands to the sleeves and tried pulling from there. This had to work, surely. I pulled back as before, and with hindsight what happened next was probably inevitable; an almighty ripping sound. The pressure around my body disappeared and I felt free. The dress was off – that was the good news. The rather worse news was that the arm of the dress had almost detached itself from the bodice. On closer inspection I saw that the bodice itself was also ripped, and the zip was hanging off.

"Oh good God, no," said Veronica as we both stared helplessly at the damaged dress.

"What should I do?"

Veronica didn't answer me, so for some considerable time we both simply stared at the dress as if we might mend it by power of concentration.

"Get dressed," said Veronica, leaving the changing room with the badly ripped dress.

Once she was gone, I clambered into my capri trousers and powder pink A-line top, relieved to be in clothes that fitted. There were welts in my skin where the tight bodice of the dress had dug in around my waist.

I checked myself in the mirror, running my hands through my blonde hair.

God, I'm so fat. I hate that I look like this.

Like anyone of large size, I'd tried every diet imaginable. The only thing that ever worked for me was Overeaters Anonymous. I'd been on their six-week introductory course a few weeks earlier, lost two stone and felt great afterwards. That was also where I met my awesome boyfriend, Ted (not quite as exciting as losing two stone, but almost). That course was also where I met Veronica and loads of other friends. I suppose you could say it changed my life. The second stage of the course started in three weeks and I couldn't bloody wait for it.

I walked out of the changing room to see Veronica standing there.

"Where's the dress?" I asked. I knew I'd have to pay for it, I just wanted to get it over with.

"I gave it to the assistant and explained that it didn't fit," she replied. "Let's go."

"I have to pay," I said, but Veronica wasn't having any of it.

"Follow me," she said.

"But I feel terrible," I said. "I ripped the dress. I should've told them."

"The dress was too small."

"No, let's be honest about this: I was too big."

"Don't worry, this sort of thing happens all the time. They won't mind one bit. Let's go and meet the girls."

Veronica took my arm in a pally fashion and led me to the coffee shop down the road. She chatted happily while we strode along, pointing out beautiful clothes in the shop windows as we went, while I spent all the time envisaging a life behind bars. I kept thinking that the woman from Zara was behind us. Every time I saw a woman in black I thought she was following me and would arrest me and I'd be locked away. And what about Ted? I'd spent a lifetime trying to find a decent boyfriend, I couldn't lose him now.

"I need to go back and buy that dress," I declared.

Veronica looked over at me. "What dress?"

"The one I tried on and ripped. I need to buy it."

"What? No you don't. Why would you buy a ripped dress that never fitted you?"

"Because I don't want to spend the rest of my life behind bars."

"You're not going to end up behind bars. What are you talking about? I used to work in a shop, that sort of thing happened all the time."

"Did it?"

"All the time."

In the coffee shop we saw Liz and Janice - another couple of survivors from the weight loss course. They were tucked away in the corner, chatting and laughing so much that they didn't see us arrive. We ordered coffee and joined them, sliding onto the long, leather bench as Liz licked the foam from her coffee off the back of her spoon.

"You're here," said Liz, finally noticing us and wrapping me in a warm embrace. "It's so lovely to see you."

"You look great." Janice reached over to hug me too.

Veronica put our coffees down on the table and was enveloped in the same affection.

"I'm dying to hear how you've got on since we last saw you," said Liz. She'd been our leader on the Fat Club course and had been a huge support to me as I fought to conquer my over-eating.

"Not too bad," I said. "Things have been going OK."

"And…?" she said. "Come on, don't be shy - what's happening between you and Ted?"

"Ah…Ted," I said, with a smile. "You don't want to know about that, do you?"

"Yes!" they chorused. "Of course we do."

"It all worked out…we're together and really, really happy."

Janice burst into applause, accompanied by Liz.

"Give us the details. You went on a date…and what happened?"

"We went out for dinner soon after he got back from his trip. Do you remember ? He was just leaving to go away for a few days as the course ended. Well, he came back, we went out for dinner and it all kind of happened after that - we met for drinks and the cinema and picnics in the park…all very romantic. We've been having a lovely time. He's so nice."

They all ahhh-ed and coo-ed as I told the story of our romance, as if I'd just produced tiny new-born kittens.

"That's so sweet," said Janice, hugging herself.

"I'm so pleased, Mary," said Liz. "You two were so obviously meant to be together, I'm really happy that it's all worked out for you. Where is he now?"

"Amsterdam," I said. "He's in bloody Amsterdam. It's the first time we've spent more than a day apart and I'm really missing him."

"What's he gone there for?" asked Liz.

"His company is trying to win a big contract in Amsterdam, Ted's gone over there to meet the managing director. He's so clever, if he pulls this deal off, it'll bring in millions to the company, and he'll definitely get a bonus and pay rise. It's amazing."

"God, that is amazing. Well done him. When's he back?"

"He's back at Heathrow tomorrow night." I gave a small squeal of excitement that made Veronica turn and look at me sharply.

"I'm excited," I said, trying to explain the mouse-like squeak. "I haven't drunk a drop of alcohol since he left, I have been really good with my diet, and trying to walk as much as possible. I want to look super gorgeous for him when he gets back from his trip tomorrow... like Audrey Hepburn or something."

"Audrey Hepburn?" queried Veronica.

"OK, maybe more Marilyn Monroe or Diana Dors."

Veronica looked at me sideways. She could be horrible sometimes.

"OK, Diana Dors' big fat older sister."

"Don't be ridiculous," said Janice. "You're a beautiful, sexy, gorgeous woman. You look exactly like Marilyn Monroe. Ted must be delighted to have you by his side."

"Thank you," I said. "I can't say I feel a great deal like Marilyn Monroe at the moment. I just tried to buy a new dress in Zara and I managed to rip the thing. It was an XXL and it was still way too small."

Liz stirred sweetener into her coffee as I spoke. Not sugar. None of us would dare touch sugar in public. It would be worse than snorting cocaine in public, or defecating on the table.

"Listen, the sizing system in Zara is completely wrong. No-one can fit into their clothes."

"I think a lot of people can, or they'd go out of business. Just not me! I had to recruit Veronica to help me escape from the damn thing."

"Ahhh," said Janice. "Done that!"

"Have you?" I asked. "I felt awful. I wanted to go back and confess and offer to buy the dress. I felt like a complete criminal just leaving it there, but Veronica told me about the time she worked in a clothes shop and everyone did things like that."

"When did you used to work in a shop?" asked Janice.

"I've never worked in a shop. But madam here needed a bit of reassuring, so I pretended that I did."

"You never worked in a shop?" Oh God, this wasn't good. I should have listened to my own instincts and just bought the goddamned dress. "I'm going back."

Now, I know what you're thinking - just let it go - but I couldn't. I know I bend the rules and I lie sometimes, but this felt like stealing. I didn't want to steal something.

So I jumped up. "I'll be back in about five minutes," I said. "Wait here for me."

"Don't be so silly," said Veronica, but it was too late. I was already on my way back there to tell an undersized, gorgeous Spanish girl who didn't appear to speak very much English that the fat woman she'd been concerned about had been unable to get into the black dress with the lace sleeves and had ripped it and therefore now wished to buy it.

What I didn't realise was that as I left the coffee shop, the girls followed me. One fat lady marching down the street heading for Zara, with three fat ladies waddling along behind. I guess there was a funny side to it. The security guy on the door certainly looked twice. He probably thought I'd multiplied.

"Hi," I said to the assistant standing by the changing rooms. It was the same woman who had enquired after my well-being earlier. She smiled in recognition, but looked a little worried. She knew that nothing in this shop would fit me.

"Could I take this dress please?" I indicated my dress on the rail.

She reached over and took it off, seeing straight away that it was ripped.

"Is no good," she said. "Is rip here. No good."

"Yes, it's good. I want to take it with the rip," I said, trying to take it out of her hands.

"No, no. Is rip," she said, slowly, thinking that her accent was the problem. She showed me the way the sleeve hung off. "Is no good."

"Yes, it's fine. I want it."

"You want no good, ripped dress?"

"Yes, I want no good, ripped dress," I confirmed. I could see she thought I was completely mad. I could also see that she had seen my friends collecting behind me, like some sort of fat army in pursuit of a broken dress.

The commotion had come to the attention of the shop manager who wandered along, dressed head-to-toe in black of course, olive skinned, of course, big brown eyes, of course. Another living example of perfect Spanish beauty.

"Is problem?" said the manager.

"No problem," I said, pointing to the dress. "I want that dress."

The lady who had been serving me explained to the manager that the dress was ripped and that was why she wouldn't give it to me.

"Ahhh," said the manageress, understanding. She turned to me. "Is ripped." She spoke in the clearest voice she could muster. "No good. Ripped."

"I know," I replied. "I'd like to buy the ripped dress."

"No possible," said the manageress. "This is rubbish now. I take it."

"I would like to buy the ripped dress," I tried, aware that any sane shopper visiting Zara that sunny afternoon would have thought I was losing my mind. "Me want ripped and broken dress. I broke the dress. I need to buy it."

"No," said the assistant, looking at me ever-so kindly. "We can order you this dress, all new, not broken."

"Come on." Veronica pulled me away. "Let's go. This Zara experiment has failed."

One by one we trooped out of the shop, watched every inch of the way by two very lovely, and very confused, Spanish ladies, clutching a ripped, black skater dress.

2. ARTISTIC ENDEAVOURS

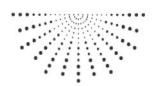

We stood on the street looking at one another, none of us quite sure what to say.

"Where shall we go?" asked Veronica.

Liz and Janice looked too shell-shocked by what they had just witnessed to be able to think of anywhere sensible to suggest.

Next to us was a small crowd, waiting to go into a white building with a large black door. The mixture of people in the queue was intriguing. Incredibly well-dressed men and women, and then what looked like a hen party of girls about my age – in their late twenties – giggling with excitement as they watched, waiting for the black door to open.

"It's going to open in less than a minute!" declared one of them.

We all stood, suddenly transfixed by the door and what it might reveal.

"Here we go," shouted another of the hen party women. "It's opening."

A man emerged wearing a jacket, black tie and white gloves. He bowed graciously and signalled for the three people at the front to go in.

"Isn't that Ashley Saunders?" I asked.

"Who?" said Veronica.

"The guy who does the travel on BBC Breakfast. You know him… always smiling and dressed in ludicrously bright coloured jackets. He's right at the front, wearing a blazer."

Veronica stared vacantly at the back of the man who delivered the news about the London traffic in the morning while Janice and Liz watched his glamorous older companion, bedecked in fur.

"I want to look like that when I'm older," said Liz.

"I wouldn't mind looking like that now," I offered. "At least she'd be able to get into the goddamned clothes in Zara."

"Are you ever going to shut up about that?" asked Veronica.

The group of younger girls was ushered through and we watched them giggle as they rushed through the door, thrilled to be granted entry into the inner sanctum.

"Come on, you come too, bring your friends," said the doorman. He was signalling to us, clearly thinking we were with the party that had just gone in.

"Come on," I said to the others. "Let's give it a try. What's the worst thing that can happen?"

Veronica gave me a stern look, but I couldn't be stopped.

"Follow me," I urged, strutting through the door.

Inside was a beautiful room with fabulous artwork all over the walls. Waiters wandered around, handing out glasses of champagne while others offered small, beautifully crafted canapés. They looked like pastry macramé. A string quartet played in the corner. It was the loveliest room I'd ever been in. A sudden wave of longing hit me and I wished like anything that Ted was standing next to me.

I wished he were right by my side, smiling down at me and gently putting his arm round me and hugging me close to him.

The four of us took a glass of champagne each, clinked our glasses together, and wandered to the side of the room to take a look at the paintings adorning the walls. Some of them were beautiful – spectacular blasts of colour and wonderful images. Others looked like they'd been done by a blind man using only his feet.

"It's so beautiful in here," said Liz. "And all the free champagne we want. How did we get invited?"

"Because we're fabulous." I winked at Liz. She smiled and regarded me with new respect, as we continued to marvel at the beautiful works of art and the immaculately dressed people wandering around, and drinking the free champagne.

"Thank you very much," I said, taking another glass and downing the whole lot in one. I was so thirsty. I know it wasn't terribly advisable to drink champagne to quench my thirst, but it seemed to be the only beverage on offer.

"Hi, yes, thank you." Another glass of champagne.

I would stop after this one. I just needed a couple of glasses to take the edge of the embarrassment of the ripped dress fiasco, then I'd rein myself in so I could look as good as possible tomorrow for the grand return of Ted.

It seemed to us, as we walked around the gallery, that the pictures nearest to the door were the more 'arty' ones. You know – they actually looked like someone painted something that exists in the world. Really lovely portraits and pictures of scenes. Further into the room sat the more modern art – piles of discarded junk with enormous price tags on them. We wandered round looking at them, but weren't wildly impressed. Perhaps they were clever, but they weren't interesting, challenging or beautiful.

"Oh, thank you, yes please." Another glass of champagne. I'd stop after this one.

Liz, Veronica and I stuck together as we walked around, trying to look as if we knew what we were talking about, while Janice wandered off deep into the gallery.

Suddenly there was a clinking of a glass, and everyone gathered towards the centre of the room where a small podium had been erected. A man in black tie stood up to it.

"Ladies and gentlemen, welcome to the Northcote Art Gallery auction. I hope you have received your brochures and have had the chance to look at all the art on sale today. We will be starting with painting one…"

And so began an auction of all the paintings, sketches and weird installations that we had been examining. I know what I'm like, so I stepped right back out of harm's way, away from the throng, so they couldn't think I was putting my hand up. I wanted to be nowhere near the people who were indicating to the auctioneer that they had £40,000 to spend on a collection of twisted up coat hangers.

I had another glass of champagne.

"Come on," said Veronica. "Let's go for a wander and find Janice."

I could see by the glassy look in Veronica's eyes and the half-smile on her lips that she'd had way too much champagne. It was probably best that we moved away from the auction. We found Janice in the back of the gallery, where the daft modern art had ended, and there was a collection of more interesting pictures on the wall.

"I like this," I observed to Veronica. "Proper art."

There was a picture by Picasso, and an odd sketch of a giraffe by Salvador Dali – mad, but really quite fun and appealing. There were also line drawings and colourful landscapes – all by artists that I'd actually heard of.

"Are these not part of the main auction?" I asked.

"This is the silent auction," said an elegant lady in black. She was stick thin. The sort of woman who would never have imagined it was possible not to fit into the biggest dress in Zara.

"Is that different from the auction out there?" I said.

"Yes, that's the public auction. Here you write down your bid and the person who writes the largest amount wins the lot."

"Oh, that sounds fun," I said. "How much has been bid so far?" I'd seen the extraordinary amounts that had been bid in the public auction, I imagined these drawings would attract millions.

"Nothing yet. They will all be along when the public auction has finished."

Veronica and I looked at the clean sheets beneath the pictures. The minimum you could bid was £5,000.

"That seems really cheap," I commented. Some of the pictures around the corner had gone for hundreds of thousands.

"Oh, they won't go for £5k, it's just the minimum you can bid.

There would be no point in bidding at that level – the financiers in there will just outbid you later."

The lady with the champagne came back again, so I finished my glass, put it onto her tray and took another one. This was the last one. Definitely the last one. Everyone was looking blurred and the art was all starting to look like it was coming off the walls.

"You know what we should do," I said to Veronica in a half-whisper. "We should bid, so we can say we bid on Picassos."

"But we can't afford £5,000," replied Veronica, quite reasonably.

"I know! We won't get them for £5,000, but at least we can tell everyone we bid. We can take a photo of the bid. It'll be so funny. Come on, come on."

This was the greatest idea ever. We put down our glasses of champagne and signed our names, placing our bets, safe in the knowledge that we would never win these works of art. It was just so funny, and the champagne was so nice. And Veronica put the picture on Facebook and everyone was commenting. We laughed a lot. Then we had more champagne, then finally, finally, we decided it was time to go home.

3. BATTERED AND BRUISED

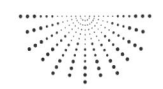

Oh Good God Alive, why do I do this to myself? Why? I clambered out of bed while a dozen men, armed with drums and drills danced and fought in my skull. I held onto the sides of my head, worried that it would split in two. All I had to do now was find a clock.

The kitchen. There was a clock in the… Shit, shit, shit, shit, shit. It was 9.15am. Bloody hell. I was supposed to get up at 7am, to be in work by 8am, but I didn't set my alarm. Of course I didn't.

I rushed to the bathroom, not letting my hands drop from the sides of my head. On the wall in the hallway there was a notice board with my LFBTTTCB campaign notes. If you're wondering what that collection of letters stands for, it's: Look Fabulous By The Time Ted Comes Back. Not catchy, but it worked. Except for this morning when it hadn't worked at all – the very day he's coming back I managed to wake up two hours late, feeling like shit.

I couldn't work out what to do. I went to the loo, brushed my teeth and sat down heavily on the edge of the bath. Everything was hurting too much for me to think properly.

On my phone there were lots of messages. One from Veronica in which she appeared to be singing, or she was being attacked and was shrieking to frighten her attackers off. It wasn't clear which.

Then there was the predictable message from work in which my sarcastic and downright miserable boss was explaining the importance of punctuality and how vital it was to call in and explain if you were going to be off. "I'm trying to run a business, Mary," he said, like I didn't know. "Please behave professionally."

Christ. I had to call in straight away. I picked up the phone and dialled the number, hoping that some excuse for why I was late would come to me before he answered.

"I had a dentist's appointment," I said. "Sorry I forgot to tell you."

"You need to have dentist's appointments in your own time," he replied firmly.

"I would have, but this was at hospital," I replied. I felt very hungover and very sick.

"At hospital? Why, what were you having done?"

And that was where it started… I invented a tale about having a back tooth removed because of an abscess in the side of my cheek and I heard him go quiet.

"It's very swollen," I said.

"I'm sorry to hear that. You should have told me," he said.

"I'll be in as soon as I can get there."

"Are you sure you're OK to come in today?"

"Yes, I'll be fine. I'm just waiting to get checked over by the nurse and then I'll be there."

"You're still in hospital?" He sounded worried and I felt very guilty.

"Yes, but I'm fine, honestly."

"OK, but don't come in unless you're sure."

I had a quick shower and dressed in my lurid green uniform that made me look like Kermit the Frog, then I rushed out of the door, forgetting my hat (yes – we had to wear green and white stripy hats because the uniforms on their own didn't make us look stupid enough). I pinned the hat to my hair and piled back out of the door, straight into Dave, the bloody gorgeous guy from the flat downstairs.

"Looking good," he said.

"Yeah right," I replied, curtseying before dashing off for the bus stop.

"You can come down tonight wearing nothing but that hat if you like."

I didn't stop to reply. There was a time, not too long ago, when I'd have been down there, wearing nothing but the hat before he could finish his sentence. No longer. I had a boyfriend, and if you hadn't realised this already – I was very fond of him.

It was 10am by the time I got into work, but everyone was too concerned about my awful dental treatment to give me much grief. They'd heard the story of abscesses and hospitals and, frankly, they were amazed to find me still alive.

"My aunt had that, it was horrific. She was off for two weeks," said Ned, the young gardener who'd joined us a few weeks ago on the apprenticeship programme.

"My aunt's face was swollen and all blue," he added, and I realised that I hadn't faked any of the swelling or discolouration that would surely accompany major dental surgery.

I should have thought about that...I could have at least held a blood-stained tissue my mouth or something. As I stood, thinking about how I might sneak out to a joke shop to buy some fake blood, an announcement came over the tannoy telling me to go and see Keith, my boss. Oh no. Now I really wished I hadn't lied. I wished I hadn't drunk so much and been such a horrible mess last night.

"Can you tell Keith I'll be there in five minutes," I said to his assistant, before I rushed out and went into the Ladies loos to do a frank appraisal of my appearance. I looked at myself in the mirror: I didn't look wonderful by any stretch of the imagination, but I didn't look as if I'd had an operation. I took a wad of hand towels from the dispenser and soaked them in water, wringing them out then moulding them into the side of my mouth to create a lump. I didn't have any blue eye shadow on me but I did have a blue mascara, so I stroked it against the back of my hand, added a little moisturiser and wiped the resulting blue crème across my cheek to create a bruise-coloured sheen. I dabbled on some pink blusher and – I swear to you – it looked bloody realistic. The paper in my cheek pushed up towards my eye, leaving that half-closed. I looked like I'd undergone some emergency operation in my mouth. It was perfect. I was a genius. I should be working in the makeup department on *Casualty*.

I left the toilets and headed to Keith's small office at the back of the centre, right next to the cafe which always smelled soooo good. I ignored the smell of bacon and had a quiet smile to myself as I remembered that I hadn't eaten anything last night, and hadn't eaten this morning. Sure, I'd drunk my way through about 40 million calories worth of alcohol, but no food. Result!

"God, Mary, you look bloody awful," said Keith when he saw me standing in his doorway. "Come in and have a sit down."

I walked slowly into his small office and sat down on one of the plastic chairs around a small round table. Every time I came into Keith's office I thought about how poorly decked out it was for the manager of a centre that sold so much lovely furniture. And why didn't he have fresh flowers in here? The gardening section was full of beautiful flowers. This room contained the sort of furniture you'd expect to find in a classroom from the 1950s.

"What the hell have they done to you?" he asked, peering at me through his very large glasses.

I couldn't talk terribly well with the paper in my mouth, and I didn't want to attempt to articulate with too much animation in case I dislodged the fake swollen cheek, so I just stood there and nodded at him and spluttered something about a dentist.

"Oh my God, your hand. Why's that so badly bruised?"

I looked down at the back of my hand. It was bright blue – like the sea when you go on holiday to Greece, like the sky on a summer's day. Not like the colour a hand should be at all.

"Is it bruised from where they put in the needle?" he asked kindly. He looked so concerned that I felt more guilty than ever. I almost wished I'd had a terrible mouth-related incident to justify such attention. I nodded at the needle question and he shook his head in dismay.

"Mary, if you had an anaesthetic this morning, you really should be taking it easier. Why don't you just keep an eye on the plants in the greenhouse today, and head off early if you need to."

I nodded.

I felt like such a fraud. I really hated lying. Hated it.

As I walked out from the meeting with Keith, my mobile rang in my pocket. I had no idea what to do. I couldn't answer it with Keith watching because I'd just given an Oscar-winning performance of a woman who couldn't speak. I pulled it out and looked at it. I didn't recognise the number and wasn't altogether sure what to do.

Keith strode out of his office and to my rescue.

"I'll get that for you, shall I?" he said, taking the phone and answering in a brisk voice: "Mary's phone. How can I help you?" The caller spoke, and Keith's eyebrows raised.

"No, Right. Yes. Of course, I'll tell her. Yes. Indeed. I'm sure she'll be delighted. Of course. Yes. Thank very much for calling."

Then he handed me the phone with a quizzical look on his face. "You've just won a secret auction," he said. "A Dali painting for five grand."

"Ohmmmmghhn," I spluttered, feeling myself turn red with embarrassment.

"You'd better call them when you're feeling better," he said. "We must be paying you too much."

4. BANNER WAVING

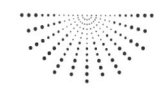

It was 7pm and I was standing at Heathrow Airport waiting for Ted to appear. He was due at any minute. The board said that his flight had landed, and that baggage was available to be collected.

"Why's it taking him so long to get his bag?" I spluttered at Veronica. I still had the paper towel in my cheek because I was terrified someone from work would see me without it and realise what a fraud I was.

"They're probably trying to find the luggage carousel, it's always miles away from the plane. It's the worst thing about flying…all the faffing around in airports.

"Yesh," I said, spluttering all over her.

Please take that out. No one from work is going to see you here. I thought the plan was for you to look as good as possible for Ted. You look like you've been bare knuckle fighting or something."

"But what if someone formwork comes? I want to keep my job."

"Take it out," she insisted. "No one's going to take your damn job away."

She could be harsh sometimes, could Veronica. Being an ex-model she openly accepted that there was a catwalk bitch tucked away inside her that emerged on occasions. Luckily, she was bloody lovely the rest of the time.

I dropped the sodden mess of tissue into my hand as surreptitiously as I could, and dropped it into my pocket. They didn't have any bins in the airport, so I was stuck with the damn thing.

"Well done," said Veronica, with a smile. "You look a lot better without it."

She had been kind enough to come with me to meet Ted because I can't drive. She stepped into the breach and said she'd take me down to meet him, then we'd all drive back together. It was very kind of her, especially after the night we'd had. We both stood there in the harsh, deeply unflattering airport lighting, feeling as wrecked as each other.

"Last night was bloody nuts," I said. "Can you believe it. We were only supposed to meet for coffee."

"I know," she said. "I woke up on the sofa with music blaring out. God know what I was doing when I got back."

I shook my head in sympathy. "And that auction. My God. What possessed us to start bidding?"

"I don't know. It seemed like such a fun thing to do at the time. What are you going to do?"

I shrugged. I didn't know. I couldn't think of anything to do other than ignore the calls from the gallery. I could no more afford to spend £5k on a piece of art than I could walk across the Thames. Let's be honest, I couldn't afford to buy a newspaper in the morning some days, never mind purchase glorious sketches from the world's greatest painters.

"We'll worry about that later," I said. "For now, I want to concentrate on Ted's homecoming. Do you think the sign's too much?"

Veronica shook her head at me. I knew she didn't think that holding up a sign was a good idea. She had already made that very clear. She hinted that it was unsophisticated and that at this stage in the relationship I should be projecting myself as classy and sophisticated.

The thing is, though, that I really wanted Ted to know how much I had missed him while he'd been away. If I rushed up to him waving a banner which said 'Welcome home, lovely Ted. I've missed you'...well, then he'd definitely know.

"Here he is," Veronica said. She sounded almost as excited as I was. We both looked over at where a line of people were walking out of the terminal. I expected Ted to be looking around and trying to see me, but he walked along sombrely, looking remarkably thoughtful and serious. I'd soon cheer him up.

"Take this," I said to Veronica, throwing my handbag at her and bounding towards Ted, trailing the banner in the air behind me and chanting the letters of his name while dancing along. I felt a thrill of love and desire run through me. How could any woman resist this gorgeous bundle of masculinity? And he was all mine. All mine!

Ted trundled along, looking care-worn and tired. Despite being several stone overweight and dressed in an ill-fitting suit, to me he looked like a superhero. My lovely, handsome, perfect Super Ted.

"Give us a 'T', give us an 'e', give us a 'd'," I shouted, shaking my wrists to flutter the banner, and smiling like a fool.

As I got close, I saw the look of horror on Ted's face. He glanced to his side at the man standing next to him. A very serious-looking man who I recognised immediately from the briefing notes that Ted had shown me. Oh God, this was the important businessman whom Ted had been to Amsterdam to visit. I stopped in my tracks just infront of them. What the hell should I do now?

With hindsight, I should just have said hello and given him a hug, but I felt really embarrassed. I was embarrassing Ted and that was the last thing I wanted to do. So, instead of greeting him warmly, I completely ignored him and went skipping off passed him as if I was heading for someone else. I continued to shout random letters as I skipped along, until I'd gone right round the arrivals hall and was almost back where I started.

Ted and the serious-looking man stood next to Veronica and watched me as I skipped along. There was no good way out of this; I'd just have to skip right up to him.

"Hello," I said nervously. "I was just doing that to help a friend. Bit too complicated to explain. All done now."

I quickly turned to the man with him. "Hello, how nice to meet you."

"Iars, this is Mary, my lovely girlfriend who I've been telling you all about."

"Oh," he said, with alarm ringing through his voice. Clearly he hadn't been expecting Ted's girlfriend to be a certifiable lunatic. "Very happy to meet. Ted is talking much about you."

"You too," I said, as we headed towards Veronica's car. This hadn't been the splendid reunion I'd hoped for, but at least Ted had been talking about me while he was away.

"What's the matter with your face?" asked Ted, as Iars and I climbed into the back of Veronica's car.

"Yes. Your cheek it is blue," said Iars.

"Yes, that's just makeup," I replied. "It's all very complicated. Don't worry"

Iars smiled and nodded, then stared at my face for the entire journey, sometimes leaning in and scrunching his eyes up to get a better look.

He was staying at the Hilton Hotel at Heathrow so we headed there first.

As we drove along, Veronica's phone rang and I saw the panic register on her face. She was a real stickler for driving sensibly and would never take a call while behind the wheel, so she passed the phone to Ted. "Would you answer that for me? It'll just be Mum – tell her I'll call her later." While my boyfriend took the phone, Veronica turned in to the hotel's driveway.

"Right," Ted was saying. "OK..."

Then he turned around and looked at Veronica quizzically. "It's some guy who says he needs to talk to you about the Picasso print you bought yesterday. He's been trying to reach you all day."

"Oh no," said Veronica, looking at me in the mirror.

That was 10 grand we needed to find between us.

5. LUNCH PLANS

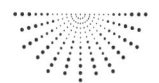

"Mary, you are bonkers," said Ted when I finished explaining to him about my ridiculous day: the ripped dress, the art exhibition and the silent auction. I told him about the fake operation and the blue makeup. I also tried to explain why I went galloping across the concourse singing his name without stopping when I saw him.

He pinched my nose affectionately and ruffled my hair. "You're very sweet," he said, and suddenly everything felt OK. Ted was absolutely perfect. He was also fatter than me which was a bloody miracle. Imagine that – his thighs were wider than mine. That had never happened before. I think I'd love him whatever his personality was like because his huge thighs make mine look small. It's a real bonus that he's a nice guy as well though.

"I've got something to ask you - what's the LFBTTTCB campaign?"

Oh God. How embarrassing. I'd meant to take that note off the wall before he got back. He must have seen it last night. "Just a think I'm doing for work," I said. He didn't know the lengths I went to in the battle to look as good as possible for him.

"So, what are you doing today then?" he asked. "Buying more art, or going to work?"

"Ha ha. Very funny. Neither. Actually, I'm not going into work today, I've got a day off, but I'm definitely not buying any more art."

"Perhaps I should join you today?" he said.

"Ooooo," I replied, looking up at him wide-eyed. "I'd love that, but don't you have to go to work?"

"I was supposed to be going to lunch with Iars and five others from the office, but it's just a social thing. The deal won't be done today."

"That would be wonderful," I squealed.

"One moment," he said, and I heard him coughing and spluttering in the hallway as he explained his sudden onset flu to his bosses.

"All sorted," he said, coming back to bed and pulling me close to him. "So what on earth are we going to do to kill the time?"

The morning flew past in a whirl of passion, cuddles and chatting. We could happily have stayed in bed all day, but hunger eventually drove us from the sheets, and I headed into the kitchen.

"I don't know what food I've got in the cupboard," I said. "I was trying to diet, so didn't really buy anything."

"We could go out to lunch?" suggested Ted.

"Oh yes, yes, yes." I was thrilled with his idea. I've always loved eating out but lunch is my favourite. Oh, and breakfast. Breakfasts are great. And brunches. Actually, I think brunches might be my favourite of all. But then dinner is delicious, isn't it, because you can have three courses at dinner, but you can't at breakfast. Why is that? It's odd really - having three courses just before going to bed, instead of in the morning when you've got the whole day ahead of you. I might mount a one woman campaign to have starters and puddings with breakfast.

"There's this lovely pub where they do enormous jacket potatoes stuffed with cheese and bacon, or why don't we go to that place with the salad bar with all the lovely coleslaws and dressings on it, and those potato wedges they do as well and the delicious steaks."

"I've got a better idea," said Ted. "Why don't we go somewhere different, somewhere we've never been before, and see whether we can discover somewhere new and fantastic."

"OK," I said. "That sounds like a good idea, but please let's not go anywhere near the garden centre. I really don't want to bump into anyone when I haven't got my swollen face on."

"We won't go anywhere near Cobham," said Ted. "Why don't we go to Putney or Barnes or somewhere like that? Let's go into London and see whether we can find somewhere wonderful to have lunch."

"Perfect," I replied.

"We don't have to go quite yet though, do we?" he said. I could feel his hands moving down my body.

"You are insatiable," I said, but inside I was delighted with the attention, the passion and adoration of this lovely man.

After 10 minutes of googling (no – that's not a euphemism) we discovered this gorgeous little place on the river in Fulham that sounded perfect. I printed off the directions, and we went in Ted's car, with me navigating. I was absolutely starving. If we didn't get there soon I'd start eating my hand.

"Left here," I shouted, sure that we could miss out loads of traffic if we went down a side road and cut out the main road.

"Good idea," said Ted, swinging the car left. "Oh look, that's Fulham Football Club."

Ted seemed to be waiting for me to comment. I didn't know what to say. I know absolutely nothing at all about football.

"We were just talking about Fulham the other day, weren't we?"

"I don't think so," I replied. "To be honest I don't think I've ever had a conversation about football with anyone in the whole world ever."

"Who on earth was I talking to about Fulham Football Club then?" he said to himself. "I can't for the life of me remember. I know someone was talking about the club."

"Can't help you, I'm afraid," I said, continuing to direct him to the pub on the river. I should point out at this stage that I have absolutely no sense of direction, I can't drive, I'm useless with maps, and I've never accurately directed anyone anywhere ever before. This was a

BERNICE BLOOM

triumph of unprecedented proportions. Ted pulled into the car parking space, put on the handbrake and smiled at me.

"We're here," he said. "You did well."

Did well? I was expecting a round of applause.

"That's the first time I've ever directed anyone and got them to the right place," I said. "Surely you have a brass band waiting to burst into a chorus of 'Congratulations'!"

"I might reward you with wine and food instead, if that's OK."

We walked into the pub garden and sat down at the table on a wooden decking area near the river. It was so beautiful. I do love London. I live on the edge of it, and should come into town more often, but it always feels like such an effort.

"I'm having the steak sandwich," said Ted after mulling over all the items on offer. I've no idea why the man looks at the menu. I've only been for a handful of meals with him but I can safely say that he always has the same thing. In one bar he spent half an hour asking questions about the dishes. "Does the chicken come with pasta? What sort of sauce is this? Would it be possible to have the braised beef with rice instead of potatoes?" Then, after he'd asked a host of questions about all the food available, he had the steak.

"I'm going for the chicken and bacon salad," I said, nobly. I wanted the fish and chips like I've never wanted anything in my life before, but I reined myself in. I could easily nick some of Ted's chips.

He headed inside to place our orders while I sat back in my seat and looked out over the river with the sun on my face. This was the most relaxed I'd been for ages. A boat chugged slowly up the river. If only life could always be like this. The gentle sounds of the water and the light, sociable chatter of people in the garden. It was lovely.

"Hide, hide..."

My silent observations were ruined by shouts from the doorway, and the sight of a large man running out of the pub towards me. I turned round to see Ted – his face a picture of tortured concentration as he tore out of the pub like Usain Bolt. He plonked the drinks down, threw himself under the table and shouted for me to get under too.

"What on earth is the matter?" I asked.

"I'll tell you in a minute. Just make sure you can't be seen."

"OK," I said, slithering underneath. "Did you order our food?"

"Yes, but then I saw Iars."

"Iars? Shit. What is he doing here?"

"He's with the guys from work, including my boss, who I lied to this morning, pretending I had flu. This is a nightmare," said Ted. "He mustn't see me. Why the hell would they bring him to this place, of all the pubs in all of London?"

"Well it is very pretty on the river, perhaps they wanted to show him a nice part of London?"

"No, damn!" Ted shook his head as we both sat crouched under the table, bent over so we wouldn't bash our heads on the wood above us. "I remember now. He's a Fulham Football Club supporter. He was the one I was talking to about the club. Damn. They must've brought him to see the ground, then taken him to lunch."

"What are we going to do?" I asked. I was full of sympathy for Ted and his plight, and I could see that he needed not to be seen by his work colleagues in the pub, but I was also bloody uncomfortable and starving. If I didn't get my chicken and bacon soon I might shrivel up and die.

"I don't know, let's stay here a bit longer, and then work out what to do."

I reached up onto the table for my glass of wine and pulled it down so I could drink it while squatting underneath the table. It would have been so much nicer to sit in the chair with the sun on my face and the view of the river, but one glance at Ted's pained face reminded me not to comment, so I sat down on the wooden decking and tried to make myself comfortable.

As we sat, chatting quietly and dearly hoping not to be seen, a gang of people came along thinking the table was empty. They pulled out the chairs and went to sit down. Ted closed his eyes and shook his head. It was all too much for him.

"Um, hello, this is our table," I said, causing a woman clutching a bottle of wine to scream and leap back.

"What are you doing there?" she asked.

I had no idea how to answer her.

"Nothing," I said. "Could you please go to a different table."

"This is ridiculous," he mouthed at me. "This is the stupidest thing ever to happen to me in my whole, entire life."

I just shrugged. It wasn't the weirdest thing to have happened to me this week, so I wasn't in a position to comment.

"One steak sandwich with fries and one chicken and bacon salad," said the waitress. She could see us under the table, but was clearly unsure where we'd want our food to be placed.

"Under here, please," said Ted, as if it was the most natural thing in the world to be sitting underneath the table in a pub on the river in Fulham.

The waitress bent down and handed us our plates and cutlery. "Shall I put the condiments here?" She pointed to the floor and we both nodded. "Is there anything else?" she asked.

I could see she was very relieved when we both said no. I was also aware that she would go straight back inside and tell the other waiters and bar staff that there were mad people in the garden, sitting under the table. Meanwhile, Ted and I sat and ate our food, like toddlers who'd had a tantrum and were refusing to sit with their parents.

"We'll see the funny side to all this soon," I said to Ted, as he tore the steak sandwich apart.

"I'm never, ever, ever pretending to be ill ever again," he replied. "I'll have to really pull out all the stops at the weekend and make this deal happen, then if they have seen me under the table they won't care, they'll just focus on the fact that I've made them a fortune."

"At the weekend?" I tried not to sound alarmed. "You have to work at the weekend?"

"Didn't I say?" he replied. "I have to go back to Amsterdam at the weekend, to try and seal this deal."

6. YOUNG MAN, YOUR TESTICLES ARE IN MY FACE

"Fancy a glass of wine?" Ted asked. "Or are you still feeling rough from yesterday."

"I'm still feeling rough from yesterday, but yes, I would really love a glass of wine," I said, as Ted ruffled my hair and walked out towards the kitchen. He took a bottle of wine from the fridge and opened it, pouring generous helpings into two large glasses.

"As a special treat, can we sit on chairs tonight and not under the table?" I asked him.

"Ha ha," he said, handing me a glass of wine. "That was nuts, wasn't it? We should have just left."

"Na, it was more fun the way we did it," I reassured him.

He kissed me on the cheek and looked deep into my eyes. "Have I told you how beautiful you are?"

"And have I told you how handsome you are?" I replied as we clinked glasses. I took a large sip and that was when I had the best idea I'd ever had in my life. Why didn't I go out to Amsterdam, and meet Ted there? I could surprise him by turning up at his hotel. As I drank more, I refined the plan in my mind. Perhaps Veronica and I could go over, and have a girly night on Friday night and Saturday,

6. YOUNG MAN, YOUR TESTICLES ARE IN MY FACE

then I could find Ted and surprise him, and we could all come back together on the Sunday. It felt like the best idea anyone had ever had.

"Where are you staying in Amsterdam?" I asked.

"Hotel Sebastian," he said. "Why?"

"No reason."

"And what are your plans while you're there?"

"Meetings during the day, dinner in the evening, then drinks in the hotel bar," he said. "Nothing too wild. Why?"

"No reason."

What could possibly go wrong?

Next morning my imaginary toothache having subsided completely, and the non-existent swelling having gone down, I was back at work. Ted's imaginary flu symptoms had disappeared as well, so he was in his office and preparing for his weekend trip to see Iars in Amsterdam. Little did he know that I was making similar plans to go to the capital of Holland.

Indeed, my day passed in a whirl of explaining to people that my injured mouth was now much better, and working out how I could get Veronica and me to Amsterdam for the least expense possible.

"By boat?" I texted to Veronica.

"Sure," she texted back. "Just as long as it's cheap."

The most economical way to travel was to get an overnight boat on Friday, followed by a train to Amsterdam on Saturday morning. It was so much cheaper than any other possible route. All we had to do was get down to the port on Friday night after work.

"I'll drive," said Veronica, and suddenly the whole thing was taking shape. The trip was cheap because we didn't need accommodation on the Friday night since we were on the boat. I just needed to find a cheap hotel room on the Saturday night and we'd be OK. But that was where I was coming unstuck. I kept rushing into the Ladies with my phone, to google hotels in Amsterdam but they were all so damn expensive.

Then Veronica stepped into the breach once more. "I have a tent," she said.

6. YOUNG MAN, YOUR TESTICLES ARE IN MY FACE

A tent? Perfect.

I booked us into a campsite and I felt a thrill of excitement run through me. We were going to bloody Amsterdam.

At 6.10pm on a busy Friday night, two very portly ladies stuffed themselves into a small Vauxhall Micra and headed for Harwich. The tent and many bags were safely stowed in the boot, along with sleeping bags and pillows. We had the tickets, passports and some hastily changed Euros, and we were off for a fun-filled weekend. We'd checked the luggage about a hundred times…the tent was there, the bags were there, and we had passport and tickets. This was going to be brilliant.

Pink came on to the radio and Veronica whacked up the volume. We were rock stars, singing along; laughing, cheering and clapping. This was going to be the best weekend of our lives. Guaranteed. And the great thing about it was that Ted had absolutely no idea we were coming. He'd have the surprise of his life and be so delighted when he saw me there. It was going to be enormous.

In the interests of subterfuge, I had resisted the urge to post anything about our trip on Facebook, in case he saw it. I'm normally the sort of person who charts her entire life through Facebook. This time I just posted:

"Quiet weekend ahead, looking forward to relaxing and doing nothing."

I got a couple of offensive comments on the post, with friends writing: "Possibly the most boring update ever on Facebook?" and "Could you be any duller, Mary?"

But they don't know… They have no idea what we are going to get up to in the land of clogs, bicycles and Edam cheese.

Veronica pulled into the car park and we clambered out and retrieved all our gear from the boot, checking it one more time: tent – check, bags – check, sleeping bags – check. We had everything. We could barely carry it all, but we had it.

Having thought that I should go for comfort rather than glamour on the boat, I now felt quite ridiculously dressed. We didn't have a

6. YOUNG MAN, YOUR TESTICLES ARE IN MY FACE

cabin so were sleeping on reclining seats, and I thought that getting to sleep would be much easier if I wore something soft and snugly. My baby pink velour onesie had seemed like the only option for guaranteed comfort, and with boots and shades, I thought I'd be able to get away with it, but now I felt stupid. Especially since Veronica was so much more soberly dressed in a white shirt and jeans. Her great poise, elegance and height could all be a bit distressing at the best of times, but more so when I'm head to foot in powder pink. Every time I caught sight of us in the shop windows I looked as if I was her overgrown toddler. I really wished I had worn something less obvious.

Hopefully my decision to opt for comfort over any semblance of style would yield rewards when it was bedtime and Veronica was struggling to get comfortable in tight jeans while I was sleeping like a baby.

We boarded the boat simply and easily, and found a good spot where we would base ourselves. Near to the bar, but not so close as to be noisy and crowded-out, near the action, but not in the centre of it.

"This has all come together much more easily than I thought it would," I said to Veronica.

"I know," she said. "To be honest, I thought it would be a miracle if we made it to the boat…let alone with all our luggage and on time!"

"We should celebrate," I declared, and Veronica gave me the thumbs up.

"Wine?"

"Yes please, my lovely," she said. "But let's try not to drink too much."

"Agreed."

We had spoken earlier in the week about how we would try our hardest not to get horribly drunk overnight on the boat. We had a big day ahead in Amsterdam, then a Saturday night with Ted. We didn't want to ruin the whole weekend because we had hangovers.

"Let's have a rule," I suggested. "For every alcoholic drink, we must have a soft one, so we alternate, and don't just drink booze all night."

"Good idea," said Veronica. "That's a really good idea. Yes." So I

6. YOUNG MAN, YOUR TESTICLES ARE IN MY FACE

went up to the bar to buy us our wines, knowing that the next round would consist of soft drinks to keep us on the straight and narrow.

We finished our first glasses, cheering as the boat left and we were on our way to the Hook of Holland. I'd soon be in the same country as Ted. It was all fiercely exciting.

Veronica went up to the bar and came back with our second drinks of the trip. You'll remember that these were supposed to be non-alcoholic but I fear that my lovely friend didn't quite understand the plan. She came back with a whole tray of drinks: soft drinks and alcoholic drinks.

"We down the soft drinks as quickly as possible, so we can get on to the wine." She plonked the tray onto the table.

"Great," I said, and this was how we proceeded through the evening, with me going to the bar next, buying two large glasses of wine and a small lemonade. We split the lemonade between two glasses and knocked it back, then carried on with the wine drinking. My great plan to cut the number of alcoholic drinks in half was failing miserably; we were just consuming sugary soft drinks as well. But we were having such a great time that it was difficult to feel too upset about it.

"What's Ted going to say when he sees us?" asked Veronica. "Will he be really shocked?"

"Definitely," I replied. Ted would be utterly thrown by our appearance. I knew him well enough to know that he'd be really pleased though. He'd be shocked and speechless, but really happy.

Veronica and I had relaxed into our new environment and were confident we could sleep in the reclining chairs, especially given how much wine we were drinking. The only thing we weren't so keen on was how young everyone on the boat was. Most of them were in their teens or early 20s, all packed around the bar knocking back shots and chasers and generally getting hammered far more quickly and more noisily than we were.

"I feel like a bloody pensioner," said Veronica, and I knew what she meant. It was a very odd experience. If there's one thing that can be

6. YOUNG MAN, YOUR TESTICLES ARE IN MY FACE

guaranteed in this world it is that when I'm drinking, I'm usually drinking more than anybody else. Look at the size of me, for goodness' sake. You don't get to my size drinking water and nibbling ice cubes.

Veronica came back from the bar with our latest trayful and plonked it down.

"This is a party boat," she said.

"What do you mean, a party boat?"

"That's what it is. It's a booze cruise and most of the people are on it are either celebrating their 18th birthday parties or 21st birthdays. No wonder we feel like two little old ladies."

"What happens on party boats?" I asked, fearing the night of debauchery ahead of us.

"According to the barman, there will be wrestling in jelly and naked bar walking later. The barman just asked me whether you were planning to enter the wet t-shirt competition later."

"Good God, is he insane?"

"I told him you wouldn't want to and he looked really disappointed."

By 3am there was no doubt that we were on a party boat. Veronica and I had tried to be good sports, we really had, but we were far too old to want to dance the night away or get fondled by amorous teenagers. I had managed to win a bottle of unbelievably disgusting 'champagne' from having a bloke's testicles dangled into my face. Before you judge me – I wasn't aware that I had agreed to this, I wasn't even aware that it was going to happen. The barman announced something, everyone started chanting and looking over at us, so I waved. Veronica smiled and waved too. We were just being friendly. Next thing, everyone was slow clapping and he shouted, "Will you?" I looked at him hopelessly and he repeated, "Come on, lady in pink – say you will."

I said "OK" fearing that I'd have to dance with an 18-year-old, but instead there was a loud cheer and a young man clambered onto the table next to our reclined seats. He pulled down his trousers, straddled my face and I had his horrible, wrinkly, teenage balls in my face before I could think straight. Then I was stuck. What could I do? Sitting up would have brought me into even closer proximity, so I closed my eyes, ignored them, and waited for him to get off. When he finally dismounted, I turned to Veronica; her eyes were out on stalks.

"What the fuck are you doing?" she asked.

"We must never speak of this again," I said. "Never."

"OK. But...what? Why did you do that? Who are you?"

"I got stuck," I said. "I was embarrassed and confused. I didn't know what to do."

The guy who'd dangled his bits in my face handed me my bottle of 'champagne', then turned to his friend. "That's the first time I've had my bollocks in a really fat girl's face," he said, and they both laughed heartily as they walked back towards the bar.

I felt like shit. I rolled over on the seat, curled up and pretend to go to sleep. I was drunk, tired and felt horrible. It was all my own fault so I wasn't looking for any sympathy, but as I closed my eyes against the wild partying on the boat, I thought about how horrible it was to be 'the fat girl' that they were all laughing at, and I started to cry.

I'd been 'the fat girl' for years. And I knew why... it was because whenever anything went even remotely wrong, I'd find myself eating huge amounts of food before I'd even realised what was happening. My mum would say something about my hair looking funny or someone at work would tell me I hadn't put the plants in the right place, and I'd feel devastated and the need to stuff myself with food until I just couldn't feel anything more would completely overwhelm me. Until I'd forced the feelings down with food, I couldn't cope. I'd feel like I'd got something missing – the resilient bit that allowed me to ignore little barbs or slights... And I suspected I knew where that came from...from an incident in a gymnastics club many years ago when I was an innocent little girl.

I wiped my eyes with the backs of my hand and tried to fall asleep before Veronica could see that I was upset. We'd soon be in Holland.

6. YOUNG MAN, YOUR TESTICLES ARE IN MY FACE

Everything would be OK. I'd lose the weight. I'd lose it and no one would ever laugh at me for being fat again.

Morning came along with all the subtlety and elegance of a nuclear missile landing on my face. The sun streamed in through the windows, lighting up the interior of the boat which, frankly, couldn't have looked in a worse state if it had crashed in the night. If you moved anything it would be tidier. There were bottles, cans, clothes and bodies lying across the seats, on the floor and on the bar. Two hardy young men still stood at the bar drinking, while all around them people had collapsed.

Two cleaners had attempted to enter the fray and were trying to impose a modicum of order over the place, but the bodies lying all over the floor prevented them from doing anything but pick up litter and collect glasses to return to the bar area. The loudspeaker announced our arrival in Holland, as Veronica and I squinted into our compact mirrors and reapplied makeup that we had never taken off the night before.

"Well, I've looked better." Veronica licked her finger and wiped it across her eyelid. "This is not a luxurious way to travel."

"No," I agreed quickly. "This booze cruise might be the worst decision we have ever made in our lives."

We joined the line of people exiting the boat, all of them looking as ropey as us. Men unshaven, women with smeared mascara across their faces, all of them piggy eyed and regretting last night's excesses.

"Right," said Veronica, putting the bags down to give her arms a break. "We can do this, all we have to do is get on the train to Amsterdam. That can't be too hard, can it?"

"It can't be," I agreed. "Once we're in Amsterdam, we can get our tent set up and relax. The hardest bit's over now."

We walked towards the train station and saw a big sign saying 'Trains to Amsterdam'.

"Brilliant," I said. Even we couldn't mess this up. All we had to do was get on the first train that came.

6. YOUNG MAN, YOUR TESTICLES ARE IN MY FACE

But Veronica had stopped and was looking open-mouthed at her bags.

"What's the matter?" I asked.

"It's the tent," she replied. "I've left it on the boat."

"Oh God no. We have to have the tent. We can't afford any of those hotels. Run back and get it and I'll wait here with the bags."

"Don't go anywhere." She turned and legged it back to the boat, weaving her way through the teenagers disembarking around her.

I had no idea whether they would allow her back on, or whether the tent would be there when she got to our seats. It might have been cleared away by the cleaners or nicked by drunk teenagers. I crossed my fingers that she would find it. We were buggered without it.

I heard Veronica running back onto the platform before I saw her. She had the tent in her arms and a look of sheer victory on her face. "Got it," she announced, holding it up like the FA Cup. "Let's go to Amsterdam."

The next train was only 10 minutes away, so we sat on the platform and talked about how much we never wanted to go on a party boat ever again.

"I've never felt so old and unadventurous before," I said.

"You were *quite* adventurous." Veronica raised her eyebrows at me.

"We said we would never speak of it," I chided.

"We won't," said Veronica. "Never."

7. MORE CAKE, PLEASE

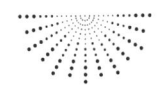

Gosh, Amsterdam was beautiful. I wasn't expecting it to be quite so stunning. I'd heard all the stories about the sex museum and prostitutes around every corner, and feared I might get drafted into some whorehouse. As it turned out it was all gorgeous waterside cafes, people cycling around without fearing for their lives, and an air of friendly sophistication. It was a joy. I loved it.

We stood on Magere Brug, otherwise known as the skinny bridge, so highly inappropriate for us two, and we looked out across the water to the little boats, sailing along, and to the cafes on the bank opposite us. I pulled out the guidebook, hoping to find out a little more about the place.

"Legend has it that the skinny bridge was named after the 'magere zussen' - the skinny sisters. They were very well-off sisters who lived either side of the river, and decided to have the wooden bridge built to make it easier to visit one another," I read.

"Maybe we should re-name Hampton Court Bridge the Fat Bridge?"

"I think we should."

"Before we do any more sight seeing, or learn about any more sisters - skinny or otherwise - I need coffee," said Veronica.

"Me too," I agreed, so we stumbled, with our many bags in hand, over the beautiful bridge and into the nearest cafe.

The weekend had got off to a captivating start, but we were both feeling the effects of last night. I felt like I'd just been through the D-Day landings as we walked along, hunched over and unwashed, desperate for a coffee. Honestly, I'd never felt so rough in my life. Well, not since the last time I felt this rough. Which, now you mention it, was only a few days ago.

"You have got the tent, haven't you?" I said to Veronica for the five hundredth time that day. She was carrying it infant of her and I was following behind, so couldn't see it. I was so paranoid after she'd left it on the boat that I felt the need to keep checking.

"Yes," she said, holding it up for me to see. "I won't lose it again. I know we're buggered without it."

We walked into the first cafe we came to...no looking at all the options and choosing the nicest. We just needed coffee inside us, and fast. The place we wandered into was just shabby-looking, with a slightly wonky canopy sitting over a small courtyard packed with metal chairs. Inside was very dark, with lots of austere-looking art on the wall.

"Two coffees, please," said Veronica in her best Dutch (obviously – no Dutch at all).

"Anything to eat?" said the waiter, his accent beautifully Dutch, but his words English.

"Oh yes please. I'm starving." Veronica looked at me nervously. "I have to eat something."

"Yes, me too," I said, nervously.

The subject of eating is always a difficult one for Veronica and me to negotiate. We met at Fat Club, for God's sake. We were only there because we had problems controlling our eating so to some extent it defined our relationship from the start. It was the ever-present third wheel in our friendship: this knowledge that we were both unable to control ourselves around food.

"What have you got that we could have for breakfast? What's typically Dutch?" I asked. "I mean – what are you famous for here?"

"Maybe this cake?" said the waiter, indicating some fairly unappetising cakes sitting in a cabinet behind him. "We are very famous for this space cake."

"Special cake? Which special cake?"

"This one."

He pointed to the unappetising cakes.

"Is it good?" I asked, unconvinced. If I was going to eat something, I wanted it to be tasty. I hated to waste calories on boring food.

"Very good indeed," he said.

"We will have two, and two cappuccinos," I said. I felt so guilty that I couldn't look at Veronica.

"Don't worry," she reassured me. "We'll get back on that diet soon."

The waiter came to our table with a tray laden with our goodies. "Enjoy," he said.

Veronica peeled a piece of the cake off and put it into her mouth. "Yum, I'm bloody starving," she said as she popped into her mouth.

I took a large sip of coffee and watched as Veronica nibbled at more of the cake.

"Is it OK?" I asked. She just shrugged, which wasn't the best recommendation in the world. Still, we needed to eat something to soak up all the alcohol still lingering within us. First, though, I needed to go to the loo.

"I'll be back in a second," I said, heading through the side door and out to the bathroom where I was entertained by a large map of Amsterdam on the door, with the key places to go circled with what looked like a bright red lipstick. I looked at them, they were all places we'd thought of going. Perhaps we should hire bicycles? Once we'd dropped our stuff off at the campsite we'd be free to cycle around all day. I rather liked the idea of that. It would be worth checking with Veronica.

But when I walked back into the cafe, Veronica was not in any fit state to discuss the hiring of bicycles. She took one look at me and burst into laughter. "Where the hell have you been?" she yelled out.

"I've just been to the loo," I replied, far more quietly than she was being. "Why are you shouting?"

"Shouting? Me?" she screamed back at me, before laughing so much she nearly fell off her chair, banging the table with her hand, as she creased over. "I've been to the loo?" she said. "I can't believe you've been to the loooooo."

What the hell was going on?

Veronica turned to the waiter who was serving the only other two people in the cafe. Thank God it was almost empty. Veronica screamed at the top of her voice: "My friend has been to the loo," before dissolving into peals of laughter again.

I sat down nervously and began to sip my coffee.

"Why are you screaming and shouting?" I asked.

"Why is your head not on properly?" she responded. "Your head is all wonky and it looks like it's going to fall off."

Before I could answer, she ran round the table and held my head between her hands. "I'm here just in time, I got here just-in-time," she said. "Your head nearly fell off. You haven't thanked me for saving it."

She rushed back to her chair, and sat back into it, nearly falling off backwards.

I nibbled at the cake, and drank my coffee while Veronica examined her thumbs, laughing occasionally about how they weren't hers at all. She wrote 'I love you' in the air with her finger and I ate my cake as quickly as possible so we could get out of there and get Veronica into the fresh air.

But no. NO. Veronica was right. It was very funny. My thumbs were on backwards too. Wooow...how did that happen?

It was so funny. I roared with laughter as I watched Veronica writing in the sky with someone else's fingers.

"Are your thumbs from a magic bird?" I asked her.

But there was no time to wait for the answer; her head was wobbling... I rushed over. Perhaps if I brushed her hair, her head would stay on her shoulders? I would try. I needed to try. But when I got to her head, the sight of all the hairs coming out of it was the funniest thing I'd ever seen. "Why have you got so much hair?" I said, laughing so much my stomach was hurting as I fell to my knees behind her, clutching a hairbrush. "You've got so much hair it's ridiculous. I'm going to count them one by one and see how many there are. I'll start at the top."

I tried to stand up in order to begin my counting but the floor was moving and I kept slipping and Veronica was laughing so much that I couldn't concentrate. Was she laughing because she had so much hair? Probably. The waiter came along and helped me to my feet, taking me to my chair and sitting me down. I looked at him and suddenly realised that he was the guy who played Superman in the film. Wow! What was he doing here?

"I need your autograph. You are Superman," I said. "How did you get to be Superman? Wow, I can't believe it, you're serving coffee and you're Superman."

"Just you have a sit down I'll bring you some water," he said.

"Go, Superman, fly through the air, get me some water."

At the next table the man and woman were looking over at us. They probably recognised the waiter as well.

"She has loads of hair all over her head and he is Superman!" I screamed across the cafe. They seemed uninterested. They just smiled at me and went back to their drinks. How could people not be interested in the fact that Superman was serving coffee?

"There you go, ladies," said the waiter, as he brought us large glasses of water. He was definitely Superman. "Next time maybe just have one hash cake between you?"

How we left the cafe is a mystery to me. I remember going to cross the road, and thinking it was really funny when the little green man appeared and collapsing into a heap. Veronica and I clutched each other in the street – howling, laughing and pointing at the little green man.

Then we seemed to have found a bench and we were sitting there, laughing. And we couldn't really move from the bench, so we closed our eyes and drifted slowly off to sleep.

We woke a couple of hours later, disorientated and confused.

"What the hell?" I asked. "I mean…what happened then?"

"Hash cake," said Veronica. "It's cake with cannabis in it. They call it space cake."

"It was the weirdest experience of my life," I said. Not particularly unpleasant, just weird. "And you do have a lot of hairs on your head."

"You are probably right," said Veronica.

It was at that point that we realised we'd lost the tent.

It fell to Veronica to return to the cafe in search of the tent, since she was the one charged with looking after it. She stood up from the bench, stumbled a little, then weaved her way across the crowded street and back to the cafe.

I dozed on the bench while she was away, to be woken up by her, grinning from ear-to-ear. She held the tent in one hand and a white paper bag in the other.

"I couldn't resist it," she said, waving her grocery bag in front of me. In it she had two more hash cakes. "Let's have these later, after we've got the tent all set up."

8. CAMPING CATASTROPHE

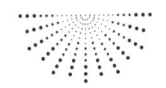

We left our bench (with the tent) and wandered of through the streets of Amsterdam in search our campsite. The more I saw of the city, the more staggeringly beautiful it appeared - a gorgeous maze of cafes, bars and canals. I'd read the literature about how lovely the city was before we went, of course, and I knew that it had more canals than Venice, but what the tourist brochure couldn't explain was just what an incredible impact those canals had on the look and feel of the place. They weaved through the city like a living, breathing animal, decorated along the route with bridges of all shapes and sizes. As we looked across the city, we could see the water snaking and gabled houses dotted along the waterfront and I had a sudden desire to come and live in the city. In fact, I might never go home. Perhaps Ted and I could move out to Amsterdam?

I pictured myself cycling around all day and losing loads of weight, then rowing down the river with Ted in the evening and meeting up with friends for supper in one of the fabulous cafes. There was such a lovely feel to the city, perhaps because it was quite small, so nowhere was too far away, and you kept seeing people you'd just met. It meant that within hours of being there, we felt like we knew people, and understood the place.

The best part of it all was the cafe culture. Cafe after cafe next to each other, with people just chilling, reading their books, and minding their own business. In England people would sit at home, watching daytime TV and feeling lonely. Here, people came out and listened to their music, read their books or chatted with passers-by. It all felt so much more healthy than the way we lived in England. Because everyone seemed to be out, there was so much to see, with people cycling past and tourists walking over the bridges, stopping to stare at the beauty of it all.

Our campsite was on the edge of town, a short bus ride from all the attractions of the city centre, and just a couple of miles, by my reckoning, from the hotel in which Ted was staying. In other words, it was perfect. It also looked clean and was buzzing as lots of people arrived and set themselves up. We went to the reception area and collected the token which allowed us to proceed.

"Here we go, we could set up here," suggested Veronica, pointing towards a lovely wide space in which we could pitch the tent and have plenty of room to sit out on deckchairs, chat and put the world to rights. It was quite near to the toilet block where we would want to go and change into our finery later, but not so close that we would be greeted by the stench of urine at all times.

"Perfect," I said, noticing no children nearby, no groups of rowdy men, and a little pathway both to the toilet block and to the exit. "I think you might have just found the most perfect place in the world."

We high-fived in our excitement.

I opened my bag which contained the sleeping bags rolled up tightly, and the small pillows that we could blow up. No luxuries had been spared. This was going to be magnificent.

"Let's get this tent set up, then we can go off and explore for a bit," said Veronica, pulling poles from the tent bag and the sheet of canvas. I looked at it all, and was filled with fear.

I remembered my own camping holidays as a child, with my parents on the brink of divorce by the time they got the tent up.

"No, that is not where it goes," my dad would howl.

"If you're so brilliant at this, why don't you just do it yourself and

I'll take the children for a walk along the beach," Mum would yell back.

"I'm not saying I'm brilliant," Dad would reply. "It's just that if you hold it there we won't be able to stretch it over the poles..." And so the arguments would continue for what felt like hours. My parents would battle with the tent, and then with one another, until finally, finally the tent was up.

But that was my parents...and I had confidence in us: Veronica and I were reasonably intelligent women, and the tent was much smaller so would be far less hassle. I looked at bits of rope, canvas and loads of poles, and I couldn't for the life of me work out how we were going to turn this collection into a beautiful tent that would house us overnight.

"Do you want to take the poles and assemble them?" Veronica said.

I couldn't help but think I'd been dealt the short straw. Wasn't it all about the poles? Wasn't I basically now in charge of the whole tent?

"I'll sort out the pegs and the canvas," she said.

I had no idea what to do. I assumed there would be enough poles to create a base square and then I would build two arches over the top onto which the canvas would be stretched, and pinned down with the pegs. But basic maths indicated that there were nowhere near enough poles for this to happen. Perhaps there was just one arch over the top?

I looked at the poles again. I couldn't see how there was even a base square let alone an arch.

"I don't really know how to do this," I said. None of the poles seemed to have bends in them. How would I make them into anything? And there were so few of them. There seemed to be a lot of string. Perhaps the string linked between the poles or something?

I turned to Veronica who was looking as puzzled as I was feeling.

"There don't seem to be enough poles," I told her. "There is a lot of string, does the string link the poles together or something? If so, we are going to need instructions because I've no idea how to do it."

"I don't know," she said in dismay. "There doesn't seem to be anything like enough canvas. And the tent is blue. I thought it was red before. I don't understand."

We stared at the poles which would no more make a tent base than I would make a nuclear scientist, and the square of canvas that wasn't big enough to make a dress. A young family walked past, nodding, smiling and wishing us a good morning, as people on campsites are prone to do.

They sounded English, so I ran over towards them, asking for help.

"I'm so sorry to interrupt your walk, but we are completely baffled here. Have you ever seen a tent like this before?" I asked. "If you could just point me in the right direction as to how it comes together, I'd be really grateful. I can't make any sense out of it."

"Sure," said the man. "I'll take a look."

I could see the woman was a bit pissed off, but we wouldn't keep them long, I just needed a steer as to how this thing came together.

A loud guffaw from the man as he looked at our collection of poles and canvas indicated that things weren't going to run smoothly from here on in.

"Is there a problem?" I asked.

The man laughed again. "Well it depends whether you want to camp tonight."

"Yes, this is our tent," I replied.

"You won't be doing any camping in this. This is a kite," he said. "It's quite a nice kite, the kids would love to come over and play with it later, if you're taking it out on the beach, but you're not going to make a tent out of it."

"Oh God," said Veronica. "I must have picked up the wrong bag. My mum said it was in the loft, so I went up and got it."

"It did seem quite small." I remembered that I had commented on how compact it was, but Veronica had said that it was the latest in modern lightweight camping equipment.

"Do you like flying kites?" she asked.

"No," I replied. "I can't think of anything I'd less like to do right now than fly a kite on the beach."

"Hash cake?" said Veronica, palming off half a cake on to me.

I looked at her and smiled. "Yep, let's eat hash cake," I replied.

And so that's how we ended up in the sex museum.

9. STATIC TENTS

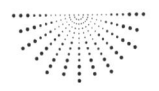

I have no idea how we got to the Sex Museum. To be honest, I've no idea why decided we wanted to go. It was never on my bucket list and, as I discovered, there were only so many times that you could witness sex acts of extraordinary weirdness in the course of a gentle afternoon in Amsterdam before you started to feel little queasy. Even when we'd had half a hash cake each and found our own feet so funny that we were crying with laughter, it still wasn't *that* entertaining.

The bizarre views on display in the museum were just obtuse. Perhaps I'm a big prude, but I don't need to see animals of different breeds at it with one another and I certainly have no desire to watch humans frolicking with farmyard beasts.

Veronica and I fumbled our way through the ground floor of the museum, then decided the escalator to the upper floors was all too much for us. Things were spinning and I'd taken against the darkness. I needed fresh air or I was going to be sick, so we staggered back through the art section, the toys section and another section which didn't seem to have any unifying theme (or any redeeming features, to be honest) and left the museum. I'm not saying we didn't enjoy it – it was fun – it was just that once you'd seen one man on all fours, bound and gagged and wearing a fake penis, you'd seen them all. You certainly didn't need to see another 20.

"What now?" asked Veronica.

"We could try and see whether there's a really cheap B&B, or youth hostel or something?" I said.

She shrugged her shoulders and raised her eyebrows in a manner which indicated that was the very last thing she wanted to do with an evening in Amsterdam.

"A bed-and-breakfast sounds better than a bloody youth hostel."

I couldn't disagree. I pulled out my phone and started googling reasonably priced B&Bs in the centre of Amsterdam. The only ones which came anywhere near the descriptor 'reasonable' were ones that were buried deep in the heart of the red-light district.

"Can you rent tents?" I asked.

"Oh, that's not a bad idea," said Veronica. "In fact, that's a very good idea. I wonder whether you can?"

Back onto Google we went. Yes, generally speaking, you could hire tents but could you hire one with no notice in the middle of Amsterdam? It seemed not. Then, I saw it.

"There's a campsite with fixed tents in it," I said. "That would be good. We wouldn't have to put it up or anything."

"Is it glamping?" asked Veronica.

"I have no idea what that is," I replied.

"It's posh camping…glamorous camping…nice tents with fridges and televisions and heating and stuff."

"Oh. I don't know. It doesn't say. It just says that the campsite we were at earlier has tents there that are permanent, so you don't have to bring one with you."

"So, the choice is – go back to the campsite and set ourselves up there, or ring Ted and explain that we're here and don't have a tent," said Veronica

It was clear that Veronica thought I should ring Ted, but we were here to surprise him. In any case, I couldn't go and see him while still dressed in a pink onesie that I'd been wearing all night.

I was also aware that Ted was working out here. He was signing a huge deal and didn't want great big distractions in the shape of Veronica and me.

"This is Ted's big break," I said to Veronica. "You know, he's worked his way up from post boy to become a really important salesman in the company, and he takes it all very seriously. When he came back from Amsterdam last time and took a day off to spend with me and felt so madly guilty about it that he's been working 20-hour days ever since. He is in Amsterdam because a big Dutch company is interested in buying his software, and if they do it'll be a multi-million pound deal for them. I can't rock up there dressed like a giant pink teddy bear and ruin it for him."

"You look fine," Veronica insisted. "Please call him or we'll end up sleeping on that bench all night."

"I haven't showered or washed my hair and I've consumed nothing but hash cakes and alcohol since midday yesterday. I don't want to see him like this."

"OK," said Veronica. "So shall we eat the other hash cake while we think about it?"

"No," I said, determinedly. "Let's go back to the campsite, get one of their fixed tents, stick our stuff in it, then eat the hash cake." I was becoming so sensible I was scaring myself.

The day was getting on. It was almost 1pm and I wanted to be looking bloody brilliant by tonight. We needed to get ourselves into the campsite and showered and changed or this whole weekend was going to collapse around our ears.

"And we should probably pick up something for lunch," I added.

"Yes," said Veronica. "Let's do that."

We nodded at one another proudly.

"We can be sensible if we try," she said.

"Yes," I agreed.

But then we ate the hash cake.

10. WE FINALLY GET TO SEE TED

At least we were in the tent when we woke up. Neither of us could remember how we got there. I had a vague memory of looking at the map and declaring that we ought to leave and find the campsite. I remembered Veronica finding this funny, of course, but then Veronica was finding everything funny by this stage. What I couldn't remember was how on earth we knew which bus to get or when to get off, or anything like that?

I could sort of remember arriving at the campsite. Yes, it was beginning to come back to me…there was a confusion at reception because we couldn't stop laughing enough to tell the man that we had booked a static tent.

"You have a tent," he said, pointing to Veronica's bag.

"It's a kite," we said, roaring with laughter. Really, everything was funny.

Somehow we made him understand that we needed a static tent, and somehow we found the right one and were now in it.

Along the way we must have bought food because two paper bags lay next to us. I sat up and pulled one towards me, waking Veronica as the paper rustled.

"I'm so starving I'm going to die," she said.

"Don't die," I replied, handing her a bag.

"Oh wow, thanks, you've been out to get food. You superstar."

"No, we bought it earlier, I think," I said. "It was here when I woke up."

It was worrying that neither of us had any recollection of buying the food, but - then - remembering anything had been a struggle since we went into the cafe this morning.

Inside the bags were sandwiches (carbs, calories), with butter on (fat, calories) and stuffed with ham and cheese (more fat, more calories and some protein), there were crisps and cans of Coke (of the non-diet variety).

Veronica and I froze as if we'd found live snakes in the bags. "Full-fat," I said.

"But we have to eat," she said. "We'll both be ill if we don't."

"OK," I said. "But this has to stay between us. We must never mention this in front of Fat Club people."

"I swear," said Veronica, solemnly. "I'll tell people about the hash cakes and the sex museum but I will never, ever talk about the full-fat Coke."

"Or what happened on the boat," I said.

"I've already forgotten about the bloke on the boat dangling his testicles in your face, so don't worry about that."

"Good," I replied.

The food was delicious. You know how utterly lovely it is to eat when you're really hungry, and oooo...we were hungry. I loved every last bit of our little picnic.

"I feel so much better now," said Veronica.

"Good, me too. Food's great, isn't it? I mean – it really is great."

Veronica nodded and pushed back her sleeve to look at her watch. "Christ. It's 4pm," she said. "How did it get to 4pm?"

"I don't know. We could do with making a plan of some sort." Veronica pulled out a map of Amsterdam.

"Right, this is where Ted is," I explained, pointing out Hotel Sebastian on the map.

Veronica marked it with a red pen.

"Here we are," I said.

She marked our campsite with her red pen.

"I think it will take us about 45 minutes to get to his hotel," I concluded.

"When should we leave?"

"Ted is going out for an early supper with Iars, the guy we met at the airport, and will be back at the hotel by 8.30pm."

"He gets back at 8.30? Are you sure? That's a really early supper," she said.

"Iars is on the red-eye to New York later, so they have to meet early. Why don't we get to his hotel while he's out at his dinner and have a few drinks in the bar, then when he comes back we scream 'surprise' and he'll be so pleased to see us he'll almost wet himself."

"That seems to me to be a simple, logical, straightforward plan." Veronica's eyes were brimming with trust and respect.

I raised my eyebrow at her.

"No, seriously," she said. "It's the sort of plan that won't go wrong."

And in that moment, something deep within me screamed: 'THE PLAN IS GOING TO GO WRONG!'

FIRST JOB WAS TO GO TO THE TOILET BLOCK TO SHOWER AND DRESS. I'd been dying for a shower all day and was starting to feel pretty revolting in my grubby, stained pink onesie, so was delighted when we made our way there and found the block clean and empty. Hooray! No queuing for the showers. We each went into a cubicle and I laid out my shower gel, shampoo, conditioner and shaving foam. I retrieved my razor from the bottom of the toiletries bag and put that on the end of the line.

"Is your shower working?" asked Veronica.

"I don't know yet." It had taken me a couple of minutes to lay out my tools. I pressed the red button and nothing happened. I turned it. Still nothing. "There's no water coming out," I shouted.

"I know," said Veronica. "I'm just trying another one but that's not working either."

Bollocks.

I slipped on my pink onesie, gathered my ruck sack and other possessions and walked outside to meet Veronica.

"What are we going to do?" I asked.

"Let's go to the reception and tell them," she said.

The reception area was busy with people chatting away in Dutch.

"Excuse me," said Veronica, spelling out her question, using mime and over-exaggerated language.

"Only seven and nine," said the man.

Veronica and I looked at one another. Neither of us had a clue what this meant.

"Showers," I tried, moving my hand above my head to mimic the falling water.

"Seven and nine, two times," said the man.

Finally a kindly English-speaking man explained. "The showers are only open between seven and nine in the morning, and seven and nine in the evening at this time of year."

"Seven?" Veronica shouted at him, as if the shower situation was wholly his fault.

"Yes," he replied. "It says it in all the literature. Most campsites are the same."

"Bugger," said Veronica. "Is there no water at all? I mean, even cold water?"

"No shower," said the man behind the counter, turning to the next person in the queue.

We walked off, back to our tent. Back to make a new plan.

We seemed to be going through plans like we were going through hash cakes…at reckless speed.

"OK," said Veronica. "We need to be showered and changed before we go out tonight."

"Yes," I agreed.

"But there are no showers here."

"Indeed not."

"So I suggest we go to Hotel Sebastian and shower there. What do you think?"

I wasn't convinced it was the greatest plan ever, but I was struggling to think of an alternative. "We'll have to get there early," I said.

"Yes, we'll get there for 6pm, then there'll be no way that we can bump into Ted because he'll already be out to supper."

"True," I said.

"We'll use the hotel showers (we'd googled this; there was a spa section in the hotel that we planned to sneak into). We'll get ready, then we'll sit in the bar, looking awesome, awaiting Ted's return."

To be honest, we'd had worse plans that day.

At 6pm we went to Hotel Sebastian and wandered in, trying to look as natural as possible and as if we were guests of the hotel just wandering around. The only problem was that we were still dressed in yesterday's yucky clothes and carrying backpacks. We didn't blend in at all with the smart Dutch women who drifted through the reception area.

"There," said Veronica, seeing a sign for the spa.

We walked over to it as nonchalantly as possible, but when Veronica tried the door it didn't open. She tried again. I tried. Nope. It wasn't opening. Suddenly it dawned on us...you needed your room key to access the spa.

There was no sign of any other showers anywhere.

"OK," said Veronica. "Don't panic. This is going to be OK. Let's just sit on this sofa and wait until someone comes to use the spa, then when they open the door, we'll pile in."

"A bit like we did with the art gallery?" I suggested.

"A bit like that."

"Because that ended up being so successful," I said.

But there was no alternative. So we sat there.

"I wish we had some hash cake," said Veronica.

"You have a problem," I said. "Forget Fat Club, you need to go to Hash Cake Club."

Then, finally, along came an elderly couple. The man flicked his room key against the lock and the door flew open. Veronica and I flew up, we dashed towards the spa and bundled in behind them, arriving just in time to get in before the door closed. Inside we were greeted by a woman in a white shirt and trousers, ticking off room numbers in the book.

"We're with them," said Veronica, pointing at the elderly couple.

"With whom?" asked the assistant.

We both looked up to point at the couple in front of us. They were disappearing into the changing area as two men walked out.

"Oh hell," Veronica said.

"Oh bloody, bloody hell," I said.

It was Ted and Iars.

OK, SO LET'S JUST SUMMARISE THE SITUATION THAT WE FOUND ourselves in…I was dressed in a dirty pink onesie, hadn't washed all day and my hair was all over the place. I'd had a conversation with Ted earlier in which I'd told him I was in Tesco's in Esher. Now, here I was, standing infront of him, about to get thrown out of a spa in Amsterdam.

Veronica and I instinctively stood still…like you're supposed to do if you see a bear in the wild. It was as if we were hoping he wouldn't notice us if we didn't flinch.

Except Ted isn't a bear, and he could see us very clearly.

"Mary, what the hell are you doing here?" he asked. "And what on earth are you wearing?"

"Oh God," I said to Veronica as quietly as I could. "I don't know what to say…"

"You need to say something," she whispered. "I'll back you up. Just say anything."

"It was all Veronica's idea," I said. But judging by the look of alarm on Veronica's face, that wasn't what she was expecting when she said 'anything'. "Veronica had to come to Amsterdam for work, so I thought I'd come with her. Sorry to take you by surprise, I was planning to call you later and see whether you wanted to meet for a drink."

I looked at Veronica, appealing with my eyes for the help she'd promised me earlier. She looked like she'd just been punched. "Yes," she said, eventually. "All my fault."

"Oh no, no one's fault at all. It's lovely to see you both. You just took us by surprise, that's all. You should have called earlier. Are you staying in this hotel?"

"No, not quite," I replied. "We had a bit of a problem with our accommodation, to be honest. The hotel that Veronica's work booked us into burned down. Completely burned to the ground. Nothing left of it – just ashes."

It was alarming how easily I was able to conjure these lies. I'd always thought myself a particularly bad liar, but it turned out that under pressure they came streaming out of me. It was a relief in many ways. It meant that if there was ever another world war and the Germans captured me, there was every chance that I'd instinctively lie and not give away the whereabouts of the British army.

"Do you two want to come up and use my room to change?" asked Ted. "I'll go and talk to the receptionist and find out which room Mark was in. He never showed up because his mum was ill, so there's a room we've paid for and aren't using."

"That's brilliant," I said, looking at Veronica, who had happily shaken off the look of utter disconsolation and was now smiling and nodding. "Then come out to dinner with Iars and myself. Is that OK, Iars?"

"Of course," he said, smiling warmly at Veronica. Ted walked over to the reception area to sort out the spare room and I looked at Veronica, blushing to the roots and glowing in the heat of Iars' stare. There was every chance we wouldn't need that room after all.

What a bloody marvellous ending to a, frankly, fraught couple of days. At least I'd learned a few things. Such as, if a tent looks too small to be a tent, it probably isn't a tent, and always watch out for the cakes in Amsterdam, they do terribly unnerving things to you.

"Right, all sorted," said Ted, returning with a key.

"This is for you," he said to Veronica, and he put his arm round me. "You, my dear, will be staying in my room."

"Oh good." I let my head rest against his shoulder as we walked along. "I'm very happy about that."

Want to know what happens next to our lovely duo?

See: **Crazy Life of an Adorable Fat Girl** to catch up with Mary and Ted as they return to Fat Club for the second course and suffer big problems in their relationship. Mary and Dave spend too much time together and the new girl at Fat Club is very alluring, and we find out what happened in Mary's past to lead her to overeating…. all in book three.

Crazy Life of an Adorable Fat Girl
OUT NOW

UK: My Book

US: My Book

MORE BOOKS

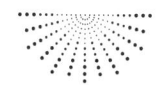

I really hope you have enjoyed reading about Mary Brown. There are loads more Adorable Fat Girl books for you to try, as she goes off on holiday, receives a mysterious invitation and tries online dating.

There's also a romance series and a 'Wags' series.

You can find out more about all the books here:

https://bernicebloom.com/

Or just click on the links below

THANK YOU SO MUCH FOR BUYING THE BOOK.

BB xxx

BOOK ONE: DIARY OF AN ADORABLE FAT GIRL

Mary Brown is funny, gorgeous and bonkers. She's also about six stone overweight. When she realises she can't cross her legs, has trouble bending over to tie her shoelaces without wheezing like an elderly chain-smoker, and discovers that even her hands and feet look fat, it's time to take action. But what action? She's tried every diet under the sun.

This is the story of what happens when Mary joins 'Fat Club' where she meets a cast of funny characters and one particular man who catches her eye.

CLICK HERE:

My Book

BOOK TWO: Adventures of an Adorable Fat Girl

Mary can't get into any of the dresses in Zara (she tries and fails. It's messy!). Still, what does she care? She's got a lovely new boyfriend whose thighs are bigger than her's (yes!!!) and all is looking well...except when she accidentally gets herself into several thousand pounds worth of trouble at the silent auction, has to eat her lunch under the table in the pub because Ted's workmates have spotted them, and suffers the indignity of having a young man's testicles dangled into her face on a party boat to Amsterdam. Oh, and then there are all the issues with the hash-cakes and the sex museum. Besides all those things - everything's fine...just fine!

CLICK HERE:

My Book

BOOK THREE: Crazy Life of an Adorable Fat Girl

The second course of 'Fat Club' starts and Mary reunites with the cast of funny characters who graced book one. But this time there's a new Fat Club member...a glamorous blonde who Mary takes against.

We also see Mary facing troubles in her relationship with the wonderful Ted, and we discover why she has been suffering from an eating disorder for most of her life. What traumatic incident in Mary's past has caused her all these problems?

The story is tender and warm, but also laugh-out-loud funny. It will resonate with anyone who has dieted, tried to keep up with any

sort of exercise programme or spent 10 minutes in a changing room trying to extricate herself from a way too-small garment that she ambitiously tried on and is now completely stuck in.
CLICK HERE:
My Book

BOOK FOUR: FIRST THREE BOOKS COMBINED
This is the first three Fat Girl books altogether in one fantastic, funny package
CLICK HERE:
My Book

BOOK FIVE: Christmas with Adorable Fat Girl
It's the Adorable Fat Girl's favourite time of year and she embraces it with the sort of thrill and excitement normally reserved for toddlers seeing jelly tots. Our funny, gorgeous and bonkers heroine finds herself dancing from party to party, covered in tinsel, decorating the Beckhams' Christmas tree, dressing up as Father Christmas, declaring live on This Morning that she's a drug addict and enjoying two Christmas lunches in quick succession. She's the party queen as she stumbles wildly from disaster to disaster. A funny little treasure to see you smiling through the festive period.
CLICK HERE:
My Book

BOOK SIX: Adorable Fat Girl shares her Weight Loss Tips
As well as having a crazy amount of fun at Fat Club, Mary also loses weight...a massive 40lbs!! How does she do it? Here in this mini book - for the first time - she describes the rules that helped her. Also included are the stories of readers who have written in to share their weight loss stories. This is a kind approach to weight loss. It's about learning to love yourself as you shift the pounds. It worked for Mary Brown and everyone at Fat Club (even Ted who can't go a day without a bag of chips and thinks a pint isn't a pint

without a bag of pork scratchings). I hope it works for you, and I hope you enjoy it.

CLICK HERE My Book

BOOK SEVEN: ADORABLE FAT GIRL ON SAFARI

Mary Brown, our fabulous, full-figured heroine, is off on safari with an old school friend. What could possibly go wrong? Lots of things, it turns out. Mary starts off on the wrong foot by turning up dressed in a ribbon bedecked bonnet, having channeled Meryl Streep from Out of Africa. She falls in lust with a khaki-clad ranger half her age and ends up stuck in a tree wearing nothing but her knickers, while sandwiched between two inquisitive baboons. It's never dull...

CLICK HERE:

My Book

BOOK EIGHT: Cruise with an Adorable Fat Girl

Mary is off on a cruise. It's the trip of a lifetime...featuring eat-all-you-can

buffets and a trek through Europe with a 96-year-old widower called Frank and a

flamboyant Spanish dancer called Juan Pedro. Then there's the desperately

handsome captain, the appearance of an ex-boyfriend on the ship, the time she's

mistaken for a Hollywood film star in Lisbon and tonnes of clothes shopping all

over Europe.

CLICK HERE:

My Book

BOOK NINE: Adorable Fat Girl Takes up Yoga

The Adorable Fat Girl needs to do something to get fit. What about yoga? I mean - really - how hard can that be? A bit of chanting, some toe touching and a new leotard. Easy! She signs up for a weekend retreat, packs up assorted snacks and heads for the countryside to get in touch with her chi and her third eye. And that's when it all goes wrong. Featuring frantic chickens, an unexpected mud bath, men in loose-fitting shorts and no pants, calamitous headstands, a new bizarre friendship with a yoga guru and a quick hospital trip.

CLICK HERE:

My Book

BOOK TEN: The first three holiday books combined

This is a combination book containing three of the books in my holiday series: Adorable Fat Girl on Safari, Cruise with an Adorable Fat Girl and Adorable Fat Girl takes up Yoga.

CLICK HERE:

My Book

BOOK ELEVEN: Adorable Fat Girl and the Mysterious Invitation

Mary Brown receives an invitation to a funeral. The only problem is: she has absolutely no idea who the guy who's died is. She's told that the deceased invited her on his deathbed, and he's very keen for her to attend, so she heads off to a dilapidated old farm house in a remote part of Wales. When she gets there, she discovers that only five other people have been invited to the funeral. None of them knows who he is either.

NO ONE GOING TO THIS FUNERAL HAS EVER HEARD OF THE DECEASED.

Then they are told that they have 20 hours to work out why they have been invited in order to inherit a million pounds.

Who is this guy and why are they there? And what of the ghostly goings on in the ancient old building?

CLICK HERE:

My Book

BOOK TWELVE Adorable Fat Girl goes to weight loss camp

Mary Brown heads to Portugal for a weight loss camp and discovers it's nothing like she expected. "I thought it would be Slimming World in the sunshine, but this is bloody torture," she says, after boxing, running, sand training (sand training?), more running, more star jumps and eating nothing but carrots. Mary wants to hide from the instructors and cheat the system. The trouble is, her mum is with her, and won't leave her alone for a second. Then there's the angry instructor with the deep, dark secret about why he left the army; and the mysterious woman who sneaks into their pool and does synchronised swimming every night. Who the hell is she? Why's she in their pool? And what about Yvonne - the slim, attractive lady who disappears every night after dinner. Where's she going? And what unearthly difficulties will Mary get herself into when she decides to follow her to find out...

CLICK HERE:

My Book

BOOK THIRTEEN: The first two weight loss books:

This is Weight loss tips and Weight loss camp together

CLICK HERE:

My Book

BOOK FOURTEEN: Adorable Fat Girl goes online dating

She's big, beautiful and bonkers, and now she's going online dating. Buckle up and prepare for trouble, laughter and total chaos.

Mary Brown is gorgeous, curvaceous and wants to find a boyfriend.

But where's she going to meet someone new? She doesn't want to hang around pubs all evening (actually that bit's not true), and she doesn't want to have to get out of her pyjamas unless really necessary (that bit's true).

There's only one thing for it - she will launch herself majestically onto the dating scene.

Aided and abetted by her friends, including Juan Pedro and best friend Charlie, Mary heads out on NINE DATES IN NINE DAYS.

She meets an interesting collection of men, including those she nicknames: Usain Bolt, Harry the Hoarder, and Dead Wife Darren.

Then just when she thinks things can't get any worse, Juan organises a huge, entirely inadvisable party at the end.

It's internet dating like you've never known it before...
CLICK HERE:
My Book

BOOK FIFTEEN: The Official Handbook for Adorable Fat Girls

This is the Ultimate Guide to being an Adorable Fat Girl. A reference book packed with life-changing advice, and some basic rules for coping in a thin world.

For example What is being fat?
Being fat is...

- Hearing the intake of breath when you sit down on someone's new deckchair. They smile, but their eyes are screaming 'For the love of God, don't sit on that. It's new and I love it and you're the size of a baby elephant and likely to rip it in two.'
- Enjoying the warm cry: "Lose some weight lardarse" as you walk down the street. Yes, that's right - life advice from passing van drivers. Excellent. Just what we all need, a bit of drive-by counselling. And the thing is - it works perfectly...as soon as someone shouts that out, I'm really inspired to go to step aerobics and eat nothing but air-dried vegetables and grated ice cubes for the next week. NOT.
- Dealing with chaffing. We'll deal with this more a little later, but - my God - how much does it hurt? As if someone has ground smashed glass into your inner thighs before coating them with vinegar

- Fearing any occasion when you may be asked to wear a seatbelt, life jacket, or harness of any kind. It won't fit. Take a look at your harness and then a quick look at my arse. How in God's name are you going to get that child-sized device over this lorry-sized body. Don't make me try. Find a bigger one.

The book has a range of sections including coping with shopping, travelling, exercise, dating and the summer... There's also a section on the issue of being overweight at work,,along with the results of an EXCLUSIVE SURVEY conducted for this book. The results and stories are staggering.

Some of the sections are funny, some are serious, some are packed with advice, others are packed with sympathy. It's your indispensable guide to coping with life in a thin world.

CLICK HERE:
My Book

SUNSHINE COTTAGE BOOKS

Also read Bernice's romantic fiction in the Sunshine Cottage series about the Lopez girls, based in gorgeous Cove Bay, Carolina.

CLICK HERE:
My Book

-

THE WAGS BOOKS

Met Tracie Martin, the crazy Wag with a mission to change the world...

CLICK HERE:
Wag's Diary
My Book

Wags in LA
My Book

Wags at the World Cup
My Book

Printed in Great Britain
by Amazon